COLE:
NINJA OF EARTH

By Greg Farshtey

SCHOLASTIC INC.
New York   Toronto   London   Auckland
Sydney   Mexico City   New Delhi   Hong Kong

ISBN 978-0-545-44995-3

LEGO the LEGO logo, the Brick and Knob configurations and the Minifigure are trademarks of the LEGO Group. © 2012 The LEGO Group. Produced by Scholastic Inc. under license from the LEGO Group.
Published by Scholastic Inc. SCHOLASTIC and associated logos are trademarks and/or registered trademarks of Scholastic Inc.

12 11 10 9 8 7 6 5 4 3 2 1   12 13 14 15 16 17/0

Printed in the U.S.A.   40
First printing, January 2012

CONTENTS

CONTENTS

FROM THE JOURNAL OF

Sensei Wu

ole is the leader of my ninja team. I did not assign him this job. To do so would have been to force him into a role he might not have been right for, and to force the others to become followers. I allowed the true natures of the four youths to shine through. It became clear that Cole's nature is to take charge in any situation.

It fits, therefore, that he is my Ninja of Earth. Like the ground beneath our feet, he is solid and steady. He puts his friends first, preferring to focus on succeeding in the

mission than gaining personal glory. He did not join my team out of a need for revenge, like Kai; or curiosity, like Zane; or a need for adventure, like Jay. No, Cole became a ninja because it was the right thing to do.

Well, perhaps that was not the only reason.

When I first met Cole, he was climbing a mountain most felt could never be climbed. He was quite surprised to find me waiting for him at the top. As I talked with him, I learned that this was not the first time he had attempted something no one else could or would do. From sailing an unexplored ocean to skiing down an iceberg to hiking through trackless jungle, if it seemed impossible, Cole would try it. Yet, success brought no real satisfaction — it simply encouraged him to look for greater challenges.

Cole has many excellent qualities. He is strong, brave, smart, and disciplined. But he

lacked purpose. He was like a razor-sharp axe, with no tree to cut down. All the things he did to push himself to his limit served no other purpose than testing his endurance. Cole needed to know that all the things he could do, all his years of training, could in some way help others. I showed him that by learning to be a ninja and mastering Spinjitzu, he could be a part of saving this world.

How has he functioned as a leader? It has not been a simple task. His three partners are strong willed, unique people, each of whom is part of the team for his own reasons. Add to that the urgency of our mission and there has been very little time for anyone to get used to functioning as a team, let alone having a leader.

Cole has handled this situation well. He never announced that he would be leading the team, for he knew that would cause an argument. Instead, he simply took command

in the field as if it was the most natural thing in the world. In the heat of battle, there was no time for the others to dispute his role. Once it became obvious that his first priorities were the mission and the safety of his friends, the others started to accept his authority.

Still, there is a darker side to all this. Cole takes his position very seriously and worries that he will let his teammates down somehow. The night before a fight, Cole rarely sleeps, preferring to stay up and plan a strategy. He trains constantly. The standards he holds himself to are far higher than those he measures others against. Cole will not tolerate any weakness, hesitation, or failure on his part.

"These guys depend on me," he once told me. "If I freeze in battle, or I give the wrong order, or I haven't planned for every possibility, maybe someone gets hurt . . . or worse. That would put the mission in jeopardy, but more than that, it would mean a friend was harmed because I wasn't smart enough or quick enough. I won't let that happen."

And so, I watch Cole with some concern. He drives himself harder than anyone I have ever known, and no man can do that for long. He will exhaust himself and that will not serve him or the team well. Even Earth will crumble if too much pressure is applied.

For now, Cole will continue on. He will try to keep Kai from charging blindly into danger. He will encourage Jay to put his inventive skills to good use. Zane may well remain a mystery to him, but Cole will try to make the Ninja of Ice feel part of the team. And just as they turn to Cole for guidance, I will try to remain someone he can go to for the same.

h, you have got to be kidding me," said Jay.

"Why would we have done such a thing as a joke?" asked Zane, honestly confused by Jay's reaction.

"We're wasting time," snapped Kai. "Get out of the way and I'll go."

"No, I'll go," said Jay. "You'll charge in and get into who knows what trouble."

"Personally," said Zane, "I think I am the logical choice to —"

"We'll all go," said Cole, steel in his voice. **"We're a team.** Time we started acting like it."

The four ninja stood on a high cliff over-looking a vast ocean. Dark clouds threatened overhead, **bolts of lightning** warning of the storm soon to come. The icy wind cut like a dagger and only Zane seemed to not feel a chill. That wasn't surprising, considering that one of Zane's hobbies was meditating at the bottom of half-frozen lakes.

The team had been successful so far, recovering two of the Four Weapons of Spinjitzu. Their quest had led them here in search of the Nunchuks of Lightning. But it wasn't the cliff or the storm or the cold that made them hesitate. It was the sight of an impossibly huge golden chain hanging in the air before their eyes. The links disappeared into the clouds far above.

There was only one way to find out where it led, and that was to climb. Cole wasn't worried about that. He was an experienced climber, after all. What concerned him was his team: Kai, always so quick to rush into

danger; Jay, constantly talking to cover his own fears; and Zane, so cold and humorless he almost seemed like he was from another planet. Each was brave and skilled, but each also wanted to be the hero on every mission. It was Cole's job to keep them working together, but it was far from easy.

Cole glanced back at Sensei Wu. The sensei nodded once. Cole turned to his team and said, "Let's go."

Leading the way, Cole began to climb. He had learned long ago not to look down or to think about how far one might fall. Doing either one would keep a person from getting very high. Behind him, the others climbed in silence.

It felt like hours had passed before Cole's head broke through the clouds and the climb was over. If the chain itself had been a startling sight, what the Ninja of Earth now saw was even more amazing. Before

his eyes were the ruins of an entire city—a *floating* city!

Cole pulled himself up and found his balance on an iron beam. The others quickly followed. "Wow," said Jay. "I wonder what the rent is like on this place."

"Fascinating," said Zane. "I have never seen anything like it. Who built it? How does it float in air? Does anyone still live here?"

"Can we save the questions?" said Kai. "The only thing that matters is the Nunchuks of Lightning. In case you've forgotten, Samukai and his skeleton crew have my sister as prisoner—and we know his warriors aren't very far behind us."

Kai took two quick steps along the beam. Suddenly, he lost his footing. Cole lunged and grabbed him before he could fall, pulling him back to safety.

"No one has forgotten anything," said Cole sharply. "But you won't do your sister any good by getting yourself hurt. Now let's search this place. The Weapon must be here somewhere."

"It would be faster if we split up," suggested Zane.

Cole shook his head. "Too dangerous, Zane, we don't know anything about this place. Now, move out, but be careful."

The ninja began to search. The city was ancient and looked like it had been abandoned for many centuries. The design of the buildings looked like nothing anyone had ever seen before, but now the structures were covered in dust and spider webs. That would not have been so bad, except—as Jay discovered, to his regret—the spiders were four feet wide with sixteen legs and **spat venom**.

There were no obvious clues as to who built the city, how, or why they left. There was no sign of any current occupants, other than the spiders, some birds, and other wildlife. Here and there were scattered bits of

rope, pieces of wood, fragments of cloth, and other items. Some of the buildings were almost completely intact, while others looked like they might fall down if anyone breathed too hard. All the while, lightning flashed overhead, as if the sky itself were angry at the trespassers in the city.

As the ninja moved farther into the city, Cole began noticing lightning symbols carved into the walls. At first, he thought they were just decoration. Then he realized that the bolts were pointing in various directions, almost like signs.

"That's it," Cole said. "The lightning carvings are pointing the way to the Nunchuks. All we have to do is follow them."

"Let's hope that's all they're pointing toward," said Jay.

The ninja moved swiftly through narrow, winding streets. At last, they reached a dead end. Before them was a vast

building made of what appeared to be marble. When Kai brushed against the stone, though, sparks flew and so did he. As he got up off the ground, he exclaimed, "What was that?"

"This is not any known type of building material," said Zane. "It's more like . . . **solid lightning** . . . but that makes no sense."

"If you expect things to make sense," chuckled Jay, "you're hanging around with the wrong people."

"We go in," said Cole. "Be careful not to touch the walls . . . and let's hope the floors aren't electrified, too."

Inside, the building was dark. Then a lightning bolt from above would suddenly illuminate it, the light streaming through holes in the roof. The floor was dirt and actually seemed to rise and fall beneath their feet. The interior walls crackled with electricity.

All four ninja could feel their hair standing on end from the energy in the air.

It was Cole who spotted the Nunchuks. They were hanging from a metal hook high upon the south wall. It didn't take a genius to know that **raw power** was flowing from the wall through the hook and if anyone touched either, it might be the last thing they ever did.

"I'll get it," said Jay. "I'm supposed to be the Ninja of Lightning, so . . ."

"No," said Cole. "Stay put. Zane, you know what to do."

Zane nodded and took a Shuriken out of his belt. He flung it at the east wall. It ricocheted off that to strike the north wall, then flashed to the west wall. Striking that, it shot for the south wall. The rotating blades sliced through the hook, and both hook and Nunchuks fell.

Jay took two steps, leaped, did a midair somersault, and caught the Weapon before

it hit the ground. He landed on his feet with a smile on his face. "Got it!"

The dirt floor suddenly heaved, knocking all four ninja off balance. Considering that the team had already run into an Earth Dragon and an Ice Dragon on their quest, Cole had a bad feeling he knew what was about to happen.

"Run!" he shouted.

Even as the ninja fled the building, a Lightning Dragon erupted from beneath the earthen floor. With a roar, it charged toward the ninja. Amazingly, it did no damage to the building. The solid "stones" of the structure turned ghostly, allowing the dragon to pass through as it pursued the heroes.

"The chain—head for the chain!" yelled Cole. Behind them, the dragon was breathing lightning bolts. One narrowly missed Cole, singeing his robe. "Kai, scout ahead, but **keep it quiet**!"

Kai moved with great stealth to the

place where the ninja had entered the city. He peered down the chain and saw armed skeleton warriors climbing up. Fortunately, they had not seen or heard him.

"We have company," he warned the other ninja.

"Great," said Jay. "Skeletons in front of us, Lightning Dragon in back—we're going to wind up sandwich meat."

Cole thought fast. "Maybe not," he said. "We just have to learn to fly."

Later, Kai, Jay, and Zane would tell Sensei Wu of their adventure while Cole secured the Nunchuks. It was the fastest job of inventing Jay had ever done. He lashed the pieces of wood together with the rope to form four frames shaped roughly like bird wings. Then he stretched the pieces of cloth across them to make crude hang gliders. Using these, the four ninja were able to escape the city with the Nunchuks, soaring right past the enraged skeletons.

"So you were the hero," said the sensei.

Jay shook his head. "No, not me . . . I mean, Zane was the one who threw the Shuriken so we could get the Weapon."

"Then Zane was the hero," said Sensei Wu.

"Well . . . Kai was the one who spotted the skeletons coming up the chain," said Zane. "If not for him, we might have climbed down into a trap."

Sensei Wu gave a slight smile. "I see. Kai was the hero, then."

Kai frowned. "No, that's not right, either. Maybe it was Cole? He suggested that Zane use his Shuriken, and that I scout for us, and that Jay come up with a way for us to fly out of there. Is that being a hero? He didn't really *do* anything . . . did he?"

Sensei Wu looked at the ninja. "Young ones, from what you have told me, Cole let the three of you use your skills to do what

you do best, rather than trying to do every-
thing himself. Sometimes, the real hero is the
one who lets others be heroes."

Kai, Jay, and Zane would think about that
for a long time.

CHAPTER 1

Cole crouched at the edge of the cliff, peering down at the skeleton camp far below. Only two skeleton warriors were posted as guards this night. The rest were sleeping, no doubt dreaming of raiding villages and frightening innocent people. Before the night was over, they would be awakened to a far worse reality.

Jay, Zane, and Kai flanked Cole. Each of the four ninja had his own ideas of how to attack the skeletons. However, despite those different opinions, they had learned to work together as a team. Sensei Wu had made

Cole the leader, a responsibility he took extremely seriously. He had to, for it was far from an easy job.

"What are we waiting for?" Kai said in a fierce whisper. "Let's go down there and **smash them**."

"We might be able to capture the lot of them and make them talk," offered Jay. "I have a new invention made just for bagging skeleton warriors."

"Impractical," Zane replied. "We have no cage in which to hold them. Far better to beat them and drive them off. Perhaps they will lead us to their headquarters in this region."

"Quiet," Cole said. "We have a plan in place. We attack from the south and herd them toward the river. One of us will spring the trap that's set there and catch one skeleton that we can try to get answers from, if any of those boneheads knows anything . . . which I doubt."

"I don't remember voting for that plan," Kai answered. "Driving them away just means they come back again later. Spinjitzu 'em into a pile of pieces and you won't have any trouble from them anymore."

Cole closed his eyes for a moment and took a deep breath. When he opened them, he looked right at Kai and said, "You are still relatively new to this team, so I will remind you how we do things. I come up with the plan and we follow it as best we can. That's to keep the three of you safe and to make sure no innocent people get hurt in our fights."

"Cole is correct," said Zane. "But it may be that someone else would be better suited to map out our strategy. It is something to consider."

Cole pointed down below. "Let's debate after the battle. Jay, you use your flying harness to distract the guards. Zane and I will mount the attack. Kai, you head to the

river and make sure one ends up in the trap."

Kai shook his head. "Change of plan," he said. An instant later, he had run off into the darkness.

CHAPTER 2

Cole wanted to call after him, but the noise would wake the skeletons. He turned back to Zane and Jay, only to find Jay was gone, too. "Where did he go?" he asked Zane.

"I assume he wished to try out his new invention before Kai 'messes things up,'" replied Zane. "I suppose they saw flaws in your plan."

"Those two," Cole began, then stopped. There was no time to be angry. Kai and Jay were putting themselves in danger. "Let's go, Zane, we have to stop them."

But Zane was gone, too.

"All right, I'll do it myself," muttered Cole.

He was about to head down the mountain when he saw a **bright flash** from below. In the sudden illumination, he could see Jay holding a large contraption that was designed to shoot lightning bolts. Unfortunately, it had shot its bolt in the wrong direction. With a startled cry, Jay went flying through the air. He crashed hard into some trees.

The light and the noise awoke all the skeletons, just as Kai charged in. Now, instead of facing two guards, he was up against a dozen. Cole knew there was no time to waste. He dashed down the winding trail that led to the camp.

By the time he got there, Kai was in the midst of battle. Cole's eyes took in the whole scene, including the skeleton warrior about to strike Kai from behind. Cole launched himself into the air, intending to bring down the skeleton with a leaping kick. But before he could land his blow, there was a harsh cracking sound off to his right.

Cole couldn't help but flick his eyes in that direction. To his horror, he saw a huge tree falling right toward him. Using all his agility, he twisted his body in midair and managed to stop his leap. He landed awkwardly on the ground and the tree followed right after, crashing into the camp just a few feet from him.

Kai was shouting in frustration. The falling tree had cut him off from his foes. Now the skeletons were fleeing toward the river. As he got to his feet, Cole spotted Zane emerging from the woods. One look at the young ninja's face told Cole that Zane had been responsible for knocking down the tree.

"This is great," Cole snapped as he helped the dazed Jay to his feet. "Well, we won't be catching any skeletons since no one was there to spring the trap. What kind of teamwork do you call that?"

"It was a stupid plan anyway," grumbled Kai. "If we had all hit them together, we could have taken the whole camp."

"Or if my invention had worked," Jay said.

"Had the tree landed six inches to the right, it would have disabled at least half the skeletons," Zane said.

Cole didn't answer. Instead, he just turned around and headed back to the ninja camp. He never looked back to see if the others were following.

CHAPTER 3

The next morning, Cole called a meeting. Sensei Wu was off meditating, so it seemed like a good time to talk to the other ninja.

"Things like last night can't happen again," he began. "Next time, someone might get killed. I'm the leader of this team, and—"

"Maybe that's the problem," Kai broke in. "Maybe we need a new leader."

"Could be, um, Kai is right," said Jay.

"I'm glad you agree with me," Kai replied, slapping Jay on the back. "Now, when I'm running things—"

"You?" Jay interrupted. "I was talking

about me. I think we need a leader who's more inventive. You kind of think with your fists."

Now it was Zane's turn to cut in. "Actually, I believe the team would benefit from a more analytical approach to things. Rushing into battle in the grip of fury is a **recipe for disaster**."

Cole abruptly stood up. "Okay. I've had it. You think it's easy leading the three of you? It's not. If one of you thinks you can do a better job, then go ahead."

With that, Cole walked away.

For a few moments, the three remaining ninja sat in uncomfortable silence. Zane was about to suggest they go after Cole when Kai spoke up.

"All right then," said the Ninja of Fire. "If that's how he feels, fine. Let's pick a new team leader."

"Okay," said Jay. "How? Should we ask Sensei Wu who should do it?"

"The sensei chose Cole," replied Zane. "It is logical that he would prefer to continue with him."

"We'll take a vote," said Kai. "The winner will be the new leader. We can even do a secret ballot."

Zane went and got three small pieces of paper and pencils. Each of the ninja wrote down a name, folded his paper, and then tossed it onto the ground in front of them. Kai did a quick shuffle of the papers. He picked them up and began to unfold the first.

"Okay, let's see who won and why I did," he said. Kai looked down at the first piece of paper and smiled as he said, "Kai."

He unfolded the second paper and his face fell. The others could see it had the name "Zane" written on it. The third paper turned out to be a vote for Jay.

"It would appear we all voted for ourselves," said Zane.

"Now what?" asked Jay.

Kai stood up. "The next mission we tackle will decide it," he said. "Whoever does the best job will be the new leader. So you guys better get some sleep tonight—you're going to need it."

Jay was the first to wake up the next morning. Before he had even opened his eyes, he noticed that it felt unusually cold. He went to pull his blanket up, but his hand found nothing. Puzzled, he lifted one eyelid and took a look. His blanket was gone.

As he sat up, Jay wondered if some animal had snuck into camp during the night and dragged off the blanket. A quick glance showed him it would have had to be a bunch of animals, and very strong ones, too. Everything in the camp—the pots and pans, the weapons, the blankets, even the wagon—was gone. The ninja had been robbed in the night.

Jay woke up Zane and Kai. Cole had been on guard duty last night, and if something like this had happened, then something worse might have happened to Cole. Together, the three ninja headed for the outskirts of the camp.

They found Cole in the tall grass. He was unconscious, but a little cold water revived him. He winced in pain as he opened his eyes and saw his three teammates.

"Ohhh, my head is pounding," said Cole. "What happened?"

"That's what we were going to ask you," said Jay. "Did someone hit you? I don't see any marks."

With some help from the others, Cole got to his feet. "I guess so. One minute I was keeping watch, the next, **bam!** I never saw or heard anyone, though. Are you guys okay?"

"Yes, but all our gear has been stolen," said Zane. "This makes no sense. If it was a skeleton warrior, would he not have harmed us rather than just taken our equipment?"

Cole shook his head. "I would have heard one of those boneheads from a mile off. I don't think this was any skeleton."

Kai noticed something buried in the tree bark next to him. Cautiously, he plucked a shuriken out of the wood. Attached to it was a note.

Kai unfolded it and read:

This is your first warning. I have taken your possessions and next I will take something much more precious from you. Your only hope is to surrender to me.
—The Phantom Ninja

Cole pulled his ninja hood off and ran his hand through his hair. "This is bad," he said. "This is very bad."

"Do you know this person?" asked Zane.

Cole shook his head. "Not personally, just by reputation. Before Sensei Wu approached any of us, he recruited an established ninja . . . or tried to. This warrior demanded gold in return for his services. When Sensei Wu said no, the Phantom Ninja didn't take it well. He vowed that Sensei would someday regret his decision . . . and it looks like today is the day."

"What are we so worried about? He's just one ninja. There are four of us. We can take him," Kai said.

"Not without a plan. Remember, it would seem he has far more experience than we do," said Zane.

Kai shrugged. "Okay, fine. So we need a plan. Who's going to make it?"

Jay folded his arms across his chest and leaned against the tree. "Well, Kai, that's usually the leader's job, isn't it?"

Almost by reflex, everyone turned to look

at Cole. He, in turn, took a couple of steps back. "Oh, no," he said. "I'm not in charge anymore, remember? One of you can do it this time . . . if you can decide who gets the honor."

Kai started walking away, beckoning for Zane and Jay to follow. "Forget it. We'll come up with a plan on our own."

Cole watched them go, a faint smile curling around the edges of his lips.

CHAPTER 5

When the ninja team reassembled a few hours later, Kai's group had the beginnings of a plan. Since there was no way to track the Phantom Ninja down, it would be necessary to lure him into a trap. Jay would act as bait in the camp, while the other ninja hid in the woods and waited to ambush their foe as soon as he showed himself.

"What if he spots the trap?" asked Cole.

"He won't," Kai replied. "Hey, we're ninja, aren't we?"

"So is he," Cole reminded the group.

As the sun set, Kai, Zane, and Cole took up positions in the woods. Jay busied himself puttering around the camp, trying to look like he wasn't waiting to be attacked. The hours dragged by. At one point, Zane almost **launched an attack** on a figure in the forest, only to discover it was a wild boar hunting for its dinner.

By midnight, even Kai was ready to admit that the trap had been a failure. Either the Phantom Ninja had spotted it, or he simply wasn't out prowling tonight. Kai started down the tree and was about to call out to the others to go back to camp when he heard Cole yelling. He couldn't make out the words, and the sound was cut off a moment later. But Kai knew where Cole had been posted and ran in that direction.

By the time he reached the spot, Cole was gone. All that remained was his black ninja hood, pinned to a tree with a dagger. A note was wrapped around the knife handle.

Zane and Jay arrived just as Kai was opening the note. By the light of Jay's torch, they read:

Sensei Wu is even more of a fool than I thought. Did you really think you could trap me with such an obvious trick? Now I am insulted. I have taken your friend Cole. Find him by the next day, and you can have him back. Otherwise, you will never see Cole again. Your first clue is to look where moss grows.

I am waiting for you.

— The Phantom Ninja

"We must find Sensei Wu," said Zane. "He must be informed."

"Right," snapped Kai. "And when he finds out why it happened, we'll be packing to go back home. No, we have to solve it ourselves. So let's think about the first clue: 'look where moss grows.' Any suggestions?"

"Trees?" offered Jay. "We're in a forest, maybe he is trying to tell us Cole is still nearby."

Zane frowned. "Too obvious. As a clue, that would tell us nothing at all."

"Moss grows on trees. We're surrounded by trees," Kai said. "Doesn't give us much of a direction."

Zane's expression suddenly brightened. "Direction? Kai, I think you have figured out the clue."

"I did?"

"Where does moss grow? Moss grows on the *north* side of trees," said Zane. "That means he's taken Cole somewhere to the north of here."

"All right, here's what we do—" Kai began.

"Wait a minute," Jay interrupted. "It was your idea to make a trap for the Phantom

Ninja, and look what happened. Now we'll try things my way."

Kai wheeled on Jay, with **anger flashing** on his features. "And what way is that?"

"I can build something that can track the Phantom Ninja. Just give me some time, and—"

Zane cut him off. "Time is not something we have, Jay. What is needed is the same kind of analysis I just used to decode the clue."

"You said *I* figured out the clue!" said Kai.

Zane nodded. "You provided a direction, quite unknowingly, but it was my knowledge of the forest that—"

"Enough!" yelled Jay. The other two ninja turned to look at him. "We only have a day to find Cole. Let's not waste it arguing. We'll head north, and when we find him, we can each come up with our own plan to save him. Okay?"

Zane and Kai nodded their agreement. Together, the three ninja set off in silence into the north woods. Although they were a team, they had never felt less like one. Yet no one wanted to be the first to admit it.

CHAPTER 6

After walking for about an hour, they came to a bridge over a raging river. The timbers in the center of the span had been **smashed**, making it impossible to pass. A note was pinned with a ninja sword to the railing of the wrecked bridge. It read:

The three of you must find a way to make it across without using Spinjitzu, or Cole will not be making it back.
— The Phantom Ninja

"We can swim it," said Zane, then added, "I think."

"Says the guy who thinks sitting at the bottom of ice-cold ponds is fun," replied Jay. "If I only had my tools and some materials . . ."

Kai looked around. To his surprise, he spotted a length of rope nearby. Not far away was some of Jay's gear. "All right, this will be easy," he said. "All I have to do is tie the rope to one of those tree limbs overhead and swing across."

Jay, poring through his gear, ignored Kai. "Great, great. With all this, I can build rocket packs and we can fly across the bridge. Piece of cake."

Zane watched the two of them, his brow knitted with concern. Then he walked over to the nearest tree and held up his torch. Looking up, he shook his head. "Kai, these tree branches are rotten. In fact, all the big branches around here are. If you try to swing

from one, it will snap and you will wind up in the river."

"I can do it," insisted Kai.

"No. You can't," Zane replied. "The amount of momentum you would need to cross the river would make it almost certain the tree branch would break."

Jay walked over, his arms full of metal parts. "We don't need him to swing any- where. It won't take me long to build the rocket packs. Isn't it kind of funny how the Phantom Ninja just dropped my gear here?"

"I don't think it was meant to be funny," said Zane. "Not at all."

Jay set to work as Kai scaled the larg- est of the nearby trees. Zane watched as Kai shimmied out onto one of the branches and started tying the rope to it. Once he was done, he climbed down the tree and gave the rope a tug.

"Kai . . ." Zane began.

"I know what I'm doing!" snapped the Ninja of Fire.

Before Zane could say anything else, Kai stood up, took the rope in both hands, and leaped into space. He soared in a beautiful arc toward the river. At the apex of his swing, there was a sound like a **huge firecracker** going off. The next instant, arms flailing, Kai was falling toward the river.

Zane took three quick steps and leaped, hoping he had calculated Kai's rate of fall correctly. He caught his teammate in mid-air and used Kai's weight to propel them into a somersault. Zane landed on the remains of the bridge, each foot precariously balanced on opposite sides of a broken railing.

"You," Zane said, calmly but breathlessly, "have put on weight."

"Put me down," said Kai, his face almost as red as his ninja garb.

"If I do, you will get wet," Zane pointed out. "I have a better idea."

With one smooth motion, Zane hurled Kai backward toward the river bank. The Ninja of Fire landed in the dirt with a grunt. Jay burst out laughing at the sight, but the look on Kai's face quickly silenced him.

"How are you progressing, Jay?" asked Zane.

Jay shrugged. "Well . . . I can build a rocket pack, but only one. There aren't enough parts here for two others. So one of us could use it to get across, but that's all."

"You go ahead, then," said Kai, back on his feet and brushing the dirt off his clothes "Find Cole. Zane and I will manage to get across somehow and catch up to you."

Jay hesitated for a moment, then he strapped on his rocket pack. He was just about to fire it up when Zane said, "Wait! We're making a mistake."

"Another one?" said Jay.

"Remember the note," Zane explained. "It said the *three* of us must find a way across the river . . . not just one. If you go over the river and we stay here, we will have failed the test, and who knows what will happen to Cole? No, we must find a way to succeed together."

Kai kicked the rope that lay on the ground. "Rope won't do us much good if the tree branches aren't strong enough to hold us."

"And Jay is not strong enough to carry both of us across," said Zane. "But we cannot just give up. There must be a way."

Jay suddenly smiled and rushed over to where Kai stood. "I think maybe there is. Quick, tie the end of the rope around your waist, Kai."

"Huh?" said Kai, but then did as he was asked. "What crazy idea do you have now?"

"Now you, Zane," said Jay, offering his friend the rope. "Tie it around you. I don't know why I didn't think of this before."

Once Kai and Zane both had the rope securely knotted around their waists, Jay took the free end of it and tied it around himself. Kai still looked puzzled, saying, "Great. Time's running out and he wants to experiment with our lives."

"No, no," said Zane. "I believe I see his idea. It will turn out to be a very good one . . . if we survive it."

"Thanks. I think," said Jay. "Now, hang on as tight as you can!"

With that, Jay fired up his rocket pack. The thrust of the engine propelled him forward toward the river. Behind him, the rope pulled tight and Kai and Zane found themselves being jerked off their feet and into the air.

"Oh, boy," yelled Kai. "How do I get off this ride?"

Zane's answer was cut off as both he and Kai realized that the other side of the cliff was fast approaching.

"Tell me you know how to land, please!" shouted Zane.

"Well, actually . . ." Jay yelled back.

As he passed over the far bank, Jay abruptly cut the power to the rocket pack. He went into a nosedive, slamming into a bunch of prickly bushes along with Zane and Kai.

"If you ever — ow! — come up with an idea like that again — **ouch!** — you won't just have the Phantom Ninja to worry about!" threatened Kai, as he pulled thorns out of his arms and legs.

"Now, Kai," Zane said gently. "The idea *did* work, and that is what counts. We made it across the river and met the Phantom's condition. Now we should—"

An arrow shot past Zane and buried itself in a nearby tree. Wrapped around the shaft was another note.

"Never mind the arrow!" shouted Kai, already on the run. "He had to be close enough to shoot it! Find him!"

The three ninja charged into the forest. They were so focused on the chase that none of them noticed the vines stretched across the path. In short order, all three had sprung traps and were hanging upside down from tree limbs high in the air.

"I think you left out the part about 'watch where you're going,'" Jay said to Kai.

"Look below!" cried Zane.

Down in the clearing stood a ninja, clad from head to toe in charcoal gray. He was looking up at his three captives and laughing. "Is this what Sensei Wu has taught you?" said the Phantom Ninja. "I suppose I must have overrated him as a ninja master."

"Just cut us down," growled Kai, "and I'll show you a few things the sensei has taught us."

"You will get yourselves down, I'm sure, hothead," the Phantom Ninja said. "But here's a clue to think about while you are up there: A man is drowning, yet not wet. Where is he?"

Before any of the ninja could answer, their nemesis had vanished back into the forest. Kai immediately began to swing back and forth on his vine until he built up enough momentum to swing his arms up toward his ankles. He grabbed the vine with one hand and with the other tore his foot loose from it. Then, he swung over to the others and repeated the process for them. After that, it was a long drop to the ground, but Sensei Wu had taught them all how to fall safely.

"When I catch up to that guy, I swear—" Kai began.

"Save it," said Jay. "That 'man drowning' is probably Cole, which means we better figure out that clue fast."

"But in what can a man drown without getting wet?" wondered Zane. "On the face of it, it does not seem to make sense."

"You can drown in sorrow," Kai said, already heading north again. The others followed along behind. "You can drown in debt."

"Somehow, I don't think Cole borrowed money from the Phantom Ninja," Jay said.

"You can drown in other things," Zane said grimly. "Grain. Dirt. Sand."

Kai turned to look at Zane. "Sand? Wait a minute, didn't Sensei Wu say something about a big patch of sand somewhere nearby?"

"No," said Jay. "I think he said *quick*sand!"

"That's it!" shouted Kai, racing through the forest now. "It has to be!"

CHAPTER 7

They had gone only a few hundred yards when they came to a clearing. About one hundred feet from where they stood was a large pool of quicksand, with a black-garbed figure half-submerged in it. The figure was motionless, no doubt trying to keep from moving too much to slow the rate of sinking.

"Cole!" yelled Jay. "We're here! **Hang on!**"

The figure in the quicksand didn't answer. *Or he can't,* thought Kai.

Jay rushed forward to save his friend. But he didn't notice the vine stretched across

his path. Fortunately for him, Kai's keen eyes spotted the danger. The Ninja of Fire leaped, bringing Jay down with a flying tackle. They fell on the vine, which triggered a hail of daggers from a nearby stand of trees. The knives whistled over the heads of the two ninja.

"You saved my life," said Jay.

Kai got up off the ground. "You were acting like me, rushing in without thinking," he said, smiling. "And only I'm allowed to act like me in this team." Kai bent down and ripped the vine free. "Now let me see if I can put this to use."

Twirling the vine over his head like a lasso, Kai threw it toward the figure in the quicksand. The end of the vine landed right in the center of the pool, but the intended target made no move to grab it. "Cole, take hold of the vine and we'll pull you out!" Kai shouted.

No response.

"Do you think perhaps he is already . . . ?" asked Zane.

Kai abruptly turned around and started walking back into the woods. "If he doesn't want to be rescued, then we shouldn't waste our time. Let's go."

"Wait a minute!" Jay exploded. "You can't just leave him to die."

"Sure, I can," said Kai.

Zane started walking away as well. "It seems the most logical thing to do."

"You're both crazy!"

Kai's voice dropped to a whisper. "Jay, shut up and start walking. Trust me."

Jay turned back to look at the pool of quicksand. He was sure the figure had sunk lower in the last few moments. How could they just leave Cole behind? But Kai and Zane seemed certain of their actions. Slowly, he started to follow them.

Their journey was halted by an axe that flew through the air and struck the ground right at Kai's feet. The three looked up to see the Phantom Ninja standing in a tree.

"Just abandoned him to die, hmmm?" he said. "What will Sensei Wu say about that?"

"We didn't abandon anyone," said Kai. "It was a dummy in that pool. Which only seems fair since all three of us are dummies, too. Right?"

"If you say so," replied the Phantom Ninja.

"First, you attack Cole and knock him out, but you don't leave a mark," said Kai. "That takes a lot of skill. I don't think even Sensei Wu could do that."

"Then, when Kai, Cole, and I were hiding in the woods, you chose Cole as your hostage," said Zane. "One has to wonder why."

"Oh, no," said Jay. "You're not saying . . . ?"

"Yes," said the Phantom Ninja. "They are." He pulled off his hood to reveal Cole's face.

"You!" exclaimed Jay.

"Him," said Kai. "Now the question is, why?"

"Simple," said Cole, as he made his way down the tree. "The three of you were questioning my leadership. Each of you thought you'd been passed over for the job for some reason. I wanted to show you that isn't true."

Cole reached the ground and walked over to them. "Zane, you had the knowledge to figure out the moss clue. Jay, you created the invention that got the team across the river. Kai, your combat skill helped you spot the trap I set, as I knew it would. All three of you have unique abilities, and you know what you can do well . . . and all three passed the challenges I expected you to."

"I think I see," said Zane. "The true role of a leader is not only to know what he does well, but to know what all the members of his team do well. Thus you know how best to employ them on a mission."

"Exactly," said Cole.

"So all that stuff about the Phantom Ninja," said Kai, "you made all that up."

Cole hesitated a moment before answering. "Well, no. I wish I had. But there really is a Phantom Ninja. He really did ask for

money to help the sensei and was turned down. But so far his **VOWS of vengeance** are just talk."

"That's a relief," said Jay. "Between Garmadon, Samukai, and the skeleton warriors, we have enough enemies to worry about. But here's the really important question: Where's our stuff?"

Cole laughed. "Back in camp. I snuck back and returned it after you left."

"We should head there, then," said Zane. "It seems we have a lot to discuss."

CHAPTER 8

The journey back to the camp was made in silence. As they entered the clearing, Cole stopped, stunned. Not only was all the gear gone from camp—again—but the campsite itself was **completely trashed**.

"Very funny, Cole," snapped Kai.

"Really, this is carrying the game too far," commented Zane.

"Wait a minute, I didn't do this," insisted Cole. "When I saw it last, the camp was intact. Someone else must have come here after I left."

"Correct," a harsh voice replied. "And that someone was me."

The four ninja turned at the same time to see another ninja. This one was garbed in charcoal gray and standing at the edge of the clearing. None of them had any doubt who he was, but they still felt a surge of disbelief. After all, how could it be?

"The Phantom Ninja?" said Jay. "You have to be kidding me."

Faster than the eye could follow, the Phantom Ninja hurled two shuriken. They hit Jay just above the shoulders, pinning the fabric of his ninja outfit to a tree.

"Does that look like a joke to you?" asked the Phantom Ninja.

"What do you want here?" demanded Cole.

"I heard someone was using my name in vain." The Phantom Ninja chuckled. "It seemed a good time to come and ask for payment. I have already taken your weapons

66

and your campsite. What else do you have that might be of value?"

Jay yanked the shurikens out of the tree. The other three ninja spread out, each ready for combat. "I think we can find something to give you," said Kai. "But you might not like it."

The Phantom Ninja leaped high in the air from a standing start, did a midair somersault, and landed on his feet in front of Kai. "Do your worst, boy."

Kai unleashed a hail of punches and kicks. The Phantom Ninja blocked all of them without even breaking a sweat. Then, spotting an opening in Kai's defenses, he landed a **sparrow strike** in Kai's midsection that left the young ninja gasping for breath.

"You have power, but no technique," said the Phantom Ninja. "You won't live long in this business."

"It is not a business to us," said Zane, closing in. "It is a duty."

This time, it was the Phantom Ninja's turn to attack. But every blow was parried by Zane with ease. Finally, the Phantom Ninja stopped and took a step back, his eyes crinkling up as he smiled beneath his hood.

"Now, you're interesting," said the warrior. "Maybe more than you know. Observant . . . I like that."

Zane said nothing. He saw no reason to inform the Phantom Ninja that he had noticed a pattern in his combat style. Whenever his opponent was about to strike with his left hand, he would drop his right shoulder a quarter of an inch. Noticing that had allowed Zane to anticipate and block his moves.

"Shall we try it again?" asked the Phantom Ninja.

"Repeating the same action and expecting a different result is the definition of insanity," answered Zane, nonetheless preparing for another round of fighting.

The Phantom Ninja took a step forward,

dropping his right shoulder. Zane prepared for a blow from his enemy's left hand. Instead, the Phantom Ninja **lashed out** with his right, felling Zane with one strike.

"No," said the Phantom Ninja, looking down at his opponent. "Insanity was thinking you could beat me."

Cole began to whirl around, using the power of Spinjitzu to transform into a tornado. "Come on, Jay. I've had enough of this guy."

Jay nodded, hurling the two shuriken even as he channeled his Spinjitzu power into an electrical whirlwind. The Phantom Ninja blocked the missiles with little effort. Cole and Jay headed for their foe from opposite directions, intending to trap him between them. But to their surprise, the Phantom Ninja also transformed into a whirlwind, rotating just as fast as they were, but in the opposite direction. When they came close, the force of his cyclone overwhelmed theirs and they were sent sprawling on the ground.

"You . . . you know Spinjitzu, too?" said Jay, stunned.

"I know a lot of things. This, for example," said the Phantom Ninja. In the next instant, he had completely disappeared.

Cole sprang to his feet. "Where did he go?"

"I don't know," said Jay, joining him. "I never saw him move."

Zane and Kai were back in the fight as well, though now there was no one to battle. "Invisibility would make an already difficult opponent . . . **unstoppable**," said Zane.

"No one is unstoppable," said Cole. "He didn't leave us any weapons, but we'll make do with what we have. Grab sticks, rocks, anything. Throw them at the spot where you last saw him."

The ninja readied their makeshift weapons. Just before they were about to throw, the Phantom Ninja reappeared right where he had been before. He took off his hood and smiled at the young men. "Well, now I see why that one is the leader. He thinks on his feet."

"Interesting illusion," said Zane. "How did you manage that?"

"Oh, it's no illusion . . . not really, not the way you mean. I simply empty my mind of all thought. In effect, I cease to exist mentally. And with no mind, no awareness of self, I disappear," the Phantom Ninja replied.

All four ninja moved in to attack. As the Phantom Ninja fended them off with little effort, he caught Jay in the midst of a flying kick and hurled him over his shoulder. "You guys should have no problem learning that one," he continued. "Emptying your minds should be a cinch for you."

Cole looked around. The other three ninja were exhausted, but continuing to fight. Their opponent was fresh and didn't even seem to be straining. At the same time, the Phantom

Ninja did not seem to be really trying to beat them so much as looking to see what they could do. One way or the other, this fight had to end soon, Cole knew. Otherwise, his team would collapse and anything might happen.

His plan was risky, but it was the only thing left to try. "Close in!" he yelled. "Don't give him room to move!"

The Phantom Ninja made no extra effort to counter as the four advanced on him. Even as they were coming at him from every side, he simply blocked their blows as he had been doing all along.

Cole waited until he and his team were almost on top of the Phantom Ninja and each other before they shouted, **"Spinjitzu! Now!"**

Before the Phantom Ninja could react, all four ninja transformed into living tornadoes. It was perhaps the most dangerous thing they had ever done, invoking the power of Spinjitzu when they were so close together.

But it was working. The force of their spinning lifted the Phantom Ninja high into the air, and kept him helpless.

Cole waited for one minute, then two, until he was sure the Phantom Ninja must be defeated. Then he signaled the others to cease their spinning. Deprived of the air pressure that was keeping him aloft, the Phantom Ninja slammed into the ground . . . and laughed, and laughed.

Cole's heart sank. Was the Phantom Ninja still ready to fight? If so, then what?

But the fallen foe made no effort to get up and attack. Instead, his laughs subsided into warm chuckles and he grinned at Cole. "I guess I lose my wager."

"Wager?" said Cole. "What wager?"

"Sensei Wu and I made a little bet. He told me about some of the tension in camp. I wagered that, even in a crisis, his team would be too fractured to follow their leader. But you four proved me wrong."

"Wait a minute," yelled Kai. "You know Sensei Wu well enough to make bets with him? I thought you two were **bitter enemies**!"

The Phantom Ninja sat up. "Oh, that's just the story we agreed to tell. See, I was a bandit, way back when, until Wu caught me. Instead of taking me to jail, he made a deal with me. I would restrict my activities to robbing other criminals, and pass any information I learned about major threats to him."

"So all this . . . ?" said Cole.

". . . was to give you guys a common enemy when you needed one," said the Phantom Ninja. "You all want to defeat the skeletons, but you have different plans of attack. That's why you aren't working well together. With me, there was no time for arguing about the best plan of action. And look what happened."

Zane helped the Phantom Ninja to his feet. "Now what?" asked the Ninja of Ice. "You ambush us, batter us, and we are supposed

to let you go free and continue a life of theft and banditry?"

The Phantom Ninja clapped Zane on the back. "That's the score, kid—unless, of course, you want to try and defeat me a second time. But I'm not sure I'd advise that."

"Why, you . . ." Kai began, taking a forceful step toward the Phantom Ninja.

"Kai, stop!" snapped Cole. "We'll take him at his word . . . for now. If we discover that he's lying to us about anything, we'll find him again. And now he knows that we can beat him."

The Phantom Ninja smiled and shook his head. "Oh, come on . . . you don't think I would be ready for that trick the next time?"

Cole walked up to his opponent, stopping when he was nose-to-nose with him. "Then we'll come up with another trick. Do you want **to take that risk**? I'm not sure I'd advise that."

The Phantom Ninja gave a slight bow.

"Enjoy the battles to come," he said to the ninja. "Tell Sensei Wu I will leave the tea I owe him in the usual spot . . . and you'll find your gear about one hundred yards behind you in the woods. Farewell!"

With that, the Phantom Ninja vanished into the woods. Kai looked like he wanted to go after him, but Cole stopped him with a look.

"Whoever he is, whatever reason he did what he did, maybe he taught us all a lesson," said Cole. "Come on, let's gather our gear . . . and then we have skeletons to track down. Right?"

Zane, Kai, and Jay looked at one another, and then at Cole. "Right!" they said together. And with that, they set off, knowing that no matter what challenge awaited them, Cole was the best leader to guide them.

JAY: NINJA OF LIGHTNING

By Greg Farshtey

SCHOLASTIC INC.
New York   Toronto   London   Auckland
Sydney   Mexico City   New Delhi   Hong Kong

No part of this publication may be reproduced in whole or in part, stored in
a retrieval system, or transmitted in any form or by any means, electronic,
mechanical, photocopying, recording, or otherwise, without written permission
of the publisher. For information regarding permission, write to Scholastic Inc.,
Attention: Permissions Department, 557 Broadway, New York, NY 10012.

ISBN 978-0-545-44995-3

LEGO the LEGO logo, the Brick and Knob configurations and the Minifigure
are trademarks of the LEGO Group. © 2012 The LEGO Group. Produced by
Scholastic Inc. under license from the LEGO Group.
Published by Scholastic Inc. SCHOLASTIC and associated logos are
trademarks and/or registered trademarks of Scholastic Inc.

12 11 10 9 8 7 6 5 4 3 2 1   12 13 14 15 16 17/0

Printed in the U.S.A.   40
First printing, January 2012

CONTENTS

FROM THE JOURNAL OF

Sensei Wu

A team needs many things in order to succeed. Unity, strength, skill, intelligence — all of these play a part. But one thing that is often overlooked is the ability to smile in the face of danger. Heroes who can find humor in even the most terrifying situations are often the ones best able to survive.

I know this well. In my time, I encountered many adventurers who were serious every moment. Few of them proved to be successful for very long. A hero has to battle too many great evils — often only the ability

to laugh at life can keep him going.

That is one of the reasons Jay is such a valuable member of my team. He is always ready with a joke, even in the middle of a battle. His sense of humor sends a message to the others that everything will be all right, no matter what danger they may face together.

Jay is a young man of many talents. Along with being the Ninja of Lightning, he cooks and has created many inventions. He loves to talk, leading Cole to refer to him as the "mouth of lightning." He seems to truly enjoy life and to see his career as a ninja as an excuse for endless adventure.

I first met Jay when he was testing out one of his inventions, a pair of wooden wings with which he was attempting to fly. Needless to say, it did not end well. I had already calculated the mass of his invention, the direction and speed of the wind, and the

speed he would need to successfully launch himself into the air. And so when his flight ended with him crashing into a billboard, I was waiting there for him.

Unlike Zane, who does not remember his past, Jay recalls it but does not wish to speak about it. I do not believe that he has some dark deed in his past that he is ashamed of. I think perhaps he came from humble beginnings and somehow believes that to be a cause for embarrassment. I cannot imagine why this would be so. A man, after all, is not measured by the wealth in his pocket but by the riches in his heart.

Of course, there is now the matter of his obvious attraction to Kai's sister, Nya. He may well wish her to believe his early life was an exciting one and the truth would be quite different. Still, if he truly cares for her, it would be best to be honest — for if she truly cares for him, she will accept him no

matter how poor he might once have been.

Jay will tell you he is a young man of many interests, but his true passion is inventing. He once told me that he has crates full of things he has created, some of which he can no longer recall the purpose of. Leave him alone for an hour with tools and raw materials, and there is no telling what you may find when you return.

The list of his inventions is long and certainly . . . unique. There is the machine that removes the core of every apple on a tree, before they are even picked; the material that can be written on as a document, or stretched to form a waterproof tent; a blanket designed to keep one cold on hot nights; and stilts that allow one to go from extremely tall to normal height at the touch of a button. (This last invention jammed on its first use, bouncing Jay between six feet and sixty feet high over one hundred times in two minutes. He said it

took him a month to stop feeling dizzy.)

Still, all his creativity, humor, and enthusiasm would mean nothing if he was not also a skilled and brave fighter. Jay once took on an entire skeleton army in the Caves of Despair to buy his friends time. He did not hesitate to do so, although it put his life in terrible danger. For him, there simply was no question — if Zane, Kai, and Cole needed him, he would do whatever he had to in order to aid them.

Jay is truly a vital member of this team. I do not believe it could succeed without him, and I am not even certain it could exist without the qualities he possesses. Although he covers his feelings with jokes, I am sure he knows how proud his friends are to fight beside him.

THE DRAGON'S ROAR

Jay was not a happy ninja.

In the last half hour, the evil Samukai had finally stolen three of the Four Weapons of Spinjitzu; Sensei Wu had vanished over a lavafall with the fourth; and Jay and his friends were unable to pursue them because Samukai and the sensei were now both in the Underworld. Sensei Wu had counted on his new ninja to protect the Weapons from Samukai, and they had failed.

That was all bad enough. But then Kai suddenly appeared actually *riding* on a Fire Dragon. The great beasts, it seemed, were

the key to following Sensei Wu. Being not truly of this world or any other, the dragons had the power to travel between Ninjago and the Underworld. First, though, the ninja would have to master riding them.

Jay immediately sensed **disaster**. He saw only one way out. "Um, Kai, since yours is already taking passengers, why can't we all ride on it?"

Kai shook his head. "Each dragon will only carry the rider connected to its element; at least, that's what the legends all say. So we each have to ride our own."

"I see two minor problems," said Zane. "First, we know nothing about riding dragons. Second, there are no dragons to ride."

"If that's what you see as 'minor' problems, I'd hate to see your idea of 'major' ones," said Jay.

"Whichever, we better find a way to solve them if we want to find the sensei and get those Weapons back from Samukai,"

said Cole. "We let ourselves be tricked. Now we have **to make things right**."

Kai patted his dragon's scaly neck. "I think this big fellow here can provide one answer, can't you, boy?"

As if in answer, the dragon lifted its massive head and let out a long, low roar that seemed to last forever. This was followed by . . . nothing. The ninja stood around uncomfortably, not wanting to question Kai's judgment. Then they heard it — answering cries coming from the north, south, and west.

Cole pointed toward the sky. "Look! Look up there!"

High above, three great dragons were circling. The Ice Dragon was the first to land, followed by the Lightning Dragon and the Earth Dragon. They seemed to look at the Fire Dragon expectantly, as if to say, "Yes, what is it you wanted?" After a moment, they looked like they were going to fly off. The

Fire Dragon growled loudly, and the other three immediately settled down.

"All right," said Kai. "Let's go."

"Wait just a second," said Jay. "How did you manage to get a dragon to let you ride it? I doubt it just let you climb aboard, unless it was looking for a potential snack on the go."

Kai shrugged. "Well, I just explained to it what the problem was . . . and it wanted to help. If Garmadon is threatening the world, it's the dragons' world, too, at least some of the time."

Jay had to admit that made sense, in a strange sort of way. Zane and Cole went right to work trying to persuade their dragons to help them. Jay's dragon looked at the ninja through narrowed eyes, as if daring him to try to be convincing.

"Right. Here goes," Jay said to himself. Meeting the dragon's gaze, he said, "Listen, there's this guy, Garmadon, and he wants to get his hands on some really powerful

weapons—stuff that could even singe your scales. So you might want to, I don't know, help stop him."

At first, the dragon did not react at all. Then it took a deep breath and exhaled, lightning bolts shooting from its mouth. **"Yiii!"** shouted Jay, barely avoiding being fried by dragon breath.

The dragon smiled and closed its eyes.

I should have known, thought Jay. *Each of us has a different talent, and Kai's is his energy and enthusiasm. He could probably talk Garmadon into giving up, if he had the chance. Zane will just make a really logical argument to the dragon until it has to give in. But me? I'll have to do this a different way.*

Jay sat down on a hillside across from the sleeping dragon and thought about what he was good at. The first thing that came to mind was making jokes. Jay had a great sense of humor and always tried to keep his friends laughing. Maybe the dragon could

use a laugh, too. *If I smelled like that, I sure could*, thought Jay.

"Hey, dragon!" Jay said loudly. The dragon opened one eye. "How can you tell if you have a dragon in your bathroom? The door won't close! How long was the dragon's vacation? Four days and three knights! How about this one? Three ninja and a dragon walk into a dojo, and—"

The Lightning Dragon swiped its **massive tail**, knocking Jay off his feet.

"That's the worst thing about dragons," muttered Jay, standing back up. "They don't know good jokes when they hear them."

Jay went back to thinking. What else was he good at? Well, he was a pretty good cook. Even the sensei seemed to like what he made over the campfire. Maybe he could make a tasty dish for the dragon.

Looking around, Jay was able to find many things for his recipe, including fruit,

nuts, and various plants he knew were safe to eat. (Giving the dragon a poisonous plant for lunch would have been a very bad idea, after all.) He mixed them all together into a huge salad and used juice from the rillberry plant for a dressing. Then he placed the whole thing in front of the dragon's nose.

One eye half opened, and the dragon peered at the meal. It took a long sniff. When it breathed out, its electric power turned the food to ash. Then it went back to sleep.

"I'll take that as a no," Jay grumbled.

"You made a salad for a dragon?" Kai asked, in disbelief.

"What's wrong with that?" said Jay. "Why, what do dragons eat?"

"Well . . . ninja," said Kai, smiling, "especially ones who serve salads."

By this time, Jay was getting discouraged. Zane was already sitting on his dragon and Kai had his practically purring. Jay did not want to wind up being left behind just

because of an uncooperative dragon.

Think! he said to himself. *There must be something you haven't tried.*

Jay had one other talent, although not everyone called it that. He was an inventor, constantly tinkering with new gadgets and testing them out. Some of them didn't work and some of them weren't very useful, but he got a lot of satisfaction out of coming up with the ideas and putting them together. Maybe he could invent something the dragon would like.

But what would a dragon need, he wondered? It already had strength, the power of flight, natural armor, claws, and in this case, the ability to breathe lightning bolts. What would make its life better?

Then he remembered the Fire Dragon's roar. What if how loud the roar was determined which dragon was listened to? What if he could give the Lightning Dragon

the loudest roar?

Jay hurried off to the cart and returned with an armful of tools and a bunch of odds and ends. He immediately set to work building a funnel-shaped device which, when spoken into, would make the sound much louder. That was nothing new, of course, but what made it unique was that it was designed to fit inside a dragon's mouth without interfering with the beast's ability to bite and chew. It wasn't perfect, he knew—after all, it was not like he was able to measure the dragon's teeth. But if it worked, he could always modify it later.

When Jay was finished, he found he faced one more problem: getting the dragon to open its mouth long enough for him to put it in. The only thing he could think of was to make the dragon so angry that it opened up to breathe more lightning at him. And that was easy to do—he just made another salad.

19

This time, the smell of the rillberry dressing made the dragon even more irritated. It opened its vast jaws and prepared to add some sizzle to the recipe. As soon as Jay saw its mouth gaping wide, he rushed forward and put his invention into place. He was finished not a second too soon as the angry dragon slammed its mouth shut and almost caught Jay.

"**ROOOOAAAARRRR,**" said the dragon, so loudly that Jay was knocked over. The other dragons whipped their heads around in shock and it seemed like the mountains shook all around. The dragon roared a few more times, but with less fury and more a sense of celebration.

"So, what do you think?" said Jay, back on his feet again. "Nobody's going to push you around again."

The dragon gave a low rumble of satisfaction that shook the ground. Then it lowered

its great head and allowed Jay to climb onto its neck. Jay couldn't help grinning as he turned to his friends.

"What are we waiting for?" he said. "We have dragons to ride!"

CHAPTER 1

Jay and Kai rode into the village on two mules. Their friend Zane would have said this was a most undignified way for ninja to travel. It was certainly true that one couldn't be particularly stealthy when riding an animal that was clumsy and loud. But Jay was more than happy for the company, especially since it was a long ride to the village.

It was almost the end of the day. The trip to the village had taken the ninja longer than expected. There were skeletons in the hills and bandits along the road. The ones the ninja couldn't evade, they'd had to fight. It

meant a few scratches here and there, but nothing more serious than that.

Up ahead, Jay saw their destination: Lee's Supplies, the only general store for miles around. The ninja would be breaking camp and moving on in a couple of days, and basic goods—food, blankets, whetstones for sharpening swords—were in short supply. Jay and Kai had been sent to purchase what the team needed, pack it on the mules, and haul it back to camp. Normally, it was a job for one ninja, but the presence of **skeletons and bandits** led Sensei Wu to send them both. Kai wasn't thrilled about going on a shopping trip and had complained loudly about the job.

Lee, a short, chubby man with a fringe of black hair, was just locking up his shop as the ninja approached. "Hi," said Jay. "My friend and I have come a long way to buy some goods. We have mules, so you can

see we're planning on making some serious purchases. Is there still time to get them
today?"

The shopkeeper turned. At the sight of
two ninja on their mules, he seemed unsure
whether to run or burst out laughing. "Um,
well . . . um . . . the shop is closed. I'll be open
again at nine tomorrow morning."

"What?" snapped Kai. "It's not even sun-
down. What kind of a shop are you running
here?"

"What my friend is trying to say," Jay cut
in, "is that we would really appreciate it if
you would stay open for a little bit longer so
we can get what we need. A long trip here
means a long trip back — the two usually go
together, you know."

Lee emphatically shook his head. "No. My
dinner is waiting. Besides, you're ninja, aren't
you? How do I know you won't take my goods
and not pay me?"

"Why, you—" Kai said hotly. "We're out there day after day **fighting skeletons** to protect folks like you."

"Skeletons?" Lee said. He seemed startled. "Well, you won't find any of those around here. This visit is a waste of your time," he said quickly.

Jay frowned. He thought everyone knew there were skeletons in the area. How had the shopkeeper missed that bit of news? Still, arguing with him was pointless. He might decide to sell them nothing at all.

"All right," said Jay. "We'll come back in the morning. Is there an inn we can stay at overnight?"

Lee shrugged. "This is a small village. The inn is right down the street."

Jay thanked him and went over to the inn with Kai. After making sure the mules were fed and quartered in the local stable, they got rooms. Dinner at the inn was some thin soup and a hunk of old bread. Jay knew he

could make better food in his sleep. In fact, he had done so once while he was sleep-walking, which hadn't amused the sensei very much.

"What brings you here, strangers?" asked Mrs. Park, the innkeeper.

"We're in town to buy some supplies from Mr. Lee," Jay replied. "Although it seems that finding Sensei Wu's phantom teapot might be an easier task," he whispered to Kai.

"Ha!" said Mrs. Park. She was sitting in a corner knitting a red and blue scarf, apparently not interested in eating her own cooking. "Watch your money, I say. Lee is a cheat. He sells bags of flour that are half full, bread long past when it's good, nails that break when you pound on them, and axes whose heads fly off at the first chop. I had to spend so much money to replace all the things I bought from him that I almost went out of business . . . I might, still."

"I'm a trader," said Din, a young man with a shock of red hair on his head. "I carry goods from place to place. Lee buys from me and promises to pay the next time I come through the village. By the time I come back again, he has sold what he has bought from me — then claims he never purchased it and owes me nothing!"

A grizzled older man in the corner, named Lu, joined the conversation. "You complain about a raindrop in the middle of a flood. Yes, Lee is a thief and a liar. But he is not the only one in this village. He has told me many stories, and were others to hear them, there would be much trouble for someone."

"What kind of stories?" asked Kai.

The old man just shook his head. "That is not for outsiders to know. We deal with our own problems here."

You don't seem to be doing it very well, thought Kai.

"Besides," the man continued, "you would seem to have problems of your own. Half the village saw you two arguing with Lee today."

"That was a misunderstanding," Jay admitted. "It wasn't like we wanted to hurt Lee."

"Speak for yourself," Kai added under his breath.

Jay decided there had been enough conversation for one night. He tucked a piece of bread into his pocket for a midnight snack, and then he and Kai went to their rooms. The beds were just mats on the floor, but both were tired after the long trip, so they quickly fell asleep.

CRASH!

Jay abruptly sat up in bed. What was that noise? It sounded like the biggest clap of thunder he had ever heard. He could hear villagers outside, all of them sounding frightened and upset. Jay rushed out of the room to see Kai already in the hallway. The two

hurried down the stairs, out the front door, and into the street.

A crowd was gathered in front of Lee's shop—or what used to be Lee's shop. The building had collapsed. As Kai and Jay approached, they heard Din shouting that Lee had been inside.

"I am his wife," a crying woman said to the ninja. "Please help! We must get him out and bring him to a doctor."

The two ninja helped clear away the debris and pulled Lee free. Lee's wife ran to her husband. She talked to him, but then he quickly passed out. He had been hit on the head by a beam and, though still alive, would not wake up. Din, Lu, Kai, and Jay carried him to the doctor's home. After an examination, the doctor said that Lee would be alright, but there was no telling when he would awaken.

"What could have made the building just fall down like that?" wondered Din.

"And what was he doing there in the middle of the night?" asked Jay. "He seemed set on closing up the shop for the night."

"We may not know the answer to your question anytime soon," Kai said to Jay. "But maybe we can solve Din's in the morning."

The next day, Jay, Kai, Din, and Lu went to inspect the remains of Lee's shop. It was no more than a pile of timbers and canvas atop scattered food, rope, tools, and other items. It looked like a **tornado** had hit the place. *Or someone who knows Spinjitzu*, thought Jay.

"Look for anything that might explain why the building fell down," said Din.

"Maybe it was just old," suggested Lu. "I doubt Lee took very good care of the place."

"Could be," agreed Jay. "But it seems kind of odd that it would come down in the middle

of the night when Lee just happened to be inside. Still, maybe it was an accident."

"Or maybe it wasn't," said Kai.

The four men began carefully searching the rubble. They pulled out pieces of timber, looked at any nails or rope that had held the building together, and generally checked for anything that looked odd.

It was Lu who made the discovery. "Look at this," he said, pointing to one of the support beams. "It's broken right in the center."

The other three came over. The wood was fractured at just the right spot to bring the beam down. Din leaned forward to examine the break more closely. "That's funny," he said. "This wasn't cut with a saw or any other kind of blade. It looks more like it was **smashed**."

Lu gave Jay and Kai a suspicious look. Then he walked away and started examining the other three support beams. All of them had a fracture in the same place. When

he reached the last one, he bent low to examine something. When he rose, he was holding something between his fingers.

"This was snagged on the wood," said Lu.

Jay, Kai, and Din looked at what he had found. They were pieces of thread, some red and some blue—the same colors as Kai's and Jay's ninja clothing.

Din pulled a dagger from his belt and took a few steps back. "All right, you two, don't make any funny moves. Your ninja tricks won't work here."

"What?!" exclaimed Jay. "You think *we* did this? Look, I'm a lot of things—a ninja, an inventor, a pilot, and an all-around charming fellow—but I don't hurt innocent people. Not even once. And as for my friend, well, he may be a hothead, but he's mostly good."

"Thanks," said Kai. "You're a big help."

"Din, put the dagger away," said Lu. He turned to the two ninja. "I don't think anything, friends. But you have to admit, it looks

suspicious. You two argued with him yesterday, and last night someone **breaks four beams** in half and brings the place down on his head . . . someone wearing clothes the same color as yours."

Jay knew Lu was right. It did look bad for them. But if they wasted time arresting the two ninja, the real attacker might get away. He only saw one hope.

"Do you know of Sensei Wu?" Jay asked.

Both men nodded. "Of course," said Lu. "He's a great hero. Who hasn't heard of him and his Spinjitzu, and that constant cup of tea he drinks?"

"Sensei Wu is our teacher. If you honor his name, I ask for a favor," said Jay. "Give us one day to investigate this crime. We promise not to leave the village. At the end of that day, if we haven't found the real attacker, we'll face whatever justice you choose."

Lu and Din looked at each other. Then Lu nodded. "All right. I've heard tales of young

ninja working with Sensei Wu, and maybe you two are some of them. But we'll be watching you — if you try to trick us, things will go very badly for you."

At Jay's request, Din gave him directions to Lee's home. As he and Kai walked away, Kai said, "Good one. Got any idea who did it?"

"Nope."

"Any idea how we'll find out in the next day?"

"Nope."

"Now I remember why I hate traveling with you," said Kai.

CHAPTER 3

Lee's was a small but comfortable place at the edge of the village. A beautiful stand of trees took up half the front yard. Mrs. Lee was working in the garden as Jay and Kai arrived.

"Hello, Mrs. Lee," said Jay.

Mrs. Lee recognized the ninja. "Hello. What brings you here?"

"We're trying to find out who caused this disaster. The evidence seems to say it wasn't an accident. Can we ask you some questions?"

Mrs. Lee invited Jay and Kai to sit on the porch. They followed her there, with Kai

pausing on the way to look more closely at the trees. The trunks were marred, as if someone had been cutting the bark. When they finally sat down with the woman, Jay could tell she had been crying. "What do you want to know?" she asked.

"Why did Mr. Lee go back to the shop that night? It was closed, wasn't it?"

"Yes," said Mrs. Lee. "He said he thought he had left a candle burning and wanted to put it out. When he didn't return, I got worried and went to look for him. That was when I saw . . ." Mrs. Lee fought back tears. "That was when I saw the store collapse."

"Did he often go out in the middle of the night like that?" asked Kai.

Mrs. Lee shook her head. "He didn't used to. But lately he has become very forgetful. He neglects to lock the shop, or he forgets to put the money away, or he can't remember if he has unpacked the goods for the next day. So he has to go back to

40

the shop at night to take care of it."

If heading back to the store has become a habit, thought Kai, *then someone could have been waiting to ambush him. Or maybe he was meeting someone?*

"I suppose he kept the records of every-thing he bought and sold at the store?" Jay asked.

"No," said Mrs. Lee. "He uses a shed out back as a little office. He keeps the records there."

"We'd like to take a look at them. But first, is there anything else you can tell us about that night?" said Jay.

Mrs. Lee dabbed at her eyes with a cloth. "There is one thing. When I first went over to him, he was still awake, and when he saw me, he whispered one word . . . then he passed out."

"What was the word?"

Mrs. Lee looked right into Jay's eyes. "**'Traitor.'** That was what he said."

41

CHAPTER 4

With Mrs. Lee's permission, Jay and Kai went into the shed out back. It was filled with dusty boxes crammed full of paper records. Jay wished Zane was here. The Ninja of Ice was much better at making sense of such things than he. Still, Jay was an inventor and he knew that sometimes you had to make do with whatever you had on hand—even if all you had was two tired ninja. He and Kai settled down and began to read.

It didn't take long for them to discover that something wasn't right with Mr. Lee's

business. Based on his records, he had a lot more goods coming in than he was selling. Yet he kept buying more and more stuff each month. He should have been out of business by now.

"Why would he buy so many goods if he hadn't sold what he already had?" wondered Jay.

"I don't know," Kai replied. "There's enough here to supply a small army. Unless . . ."

Suddenly, there came the sound of breaking glass. Someone had thrown something through the shed window. To their shock, the ninja saw it was a burning stick. The flames jumped from the stick to one of the piles of paper, which immediately began to catch fire. Soon, the shed was full of smoke as flames spread everywhere.

Jay rushed to the door, but someone had locked it from the outside.

"The window is already blocked by fire," said Kai. "We're trapped!"

Think! Jay said to himself. *Sensei Wu didn't spend all that time training you for it to end this way. There has to be a way out.*

By now, Jay and Kai were surrounded by fire. The shed had no basement, which left only one direction open to them — straight up — and only one way to reach it.

"**Spinjitzu!**" both ninja said at the same time.

Jay and Kai began to spin, faster and faster, until anyone watching would have seen them as little more than blurs. Where once had stood two ninja, now there were living tornadoes studded with lightning bolts and fire, respectively. Slowly at first, the whirlwinds began to rise from the floor. Then they abruptly shot up, smashing a hole in the shed roof.

Jay and Kai whirled into the open air as tongues of flame and smoke pursued them through the gap in the roof. They veered sharply to the right and dropped, their spins

halting abruptly just moments before they slammed into the ground. As Kai lifted his head from the soft earth, he could see a few villagers running toward the shed.

Too late, Kai thought, as he watched the structure burn. *Any evidence is just ashes now. We'll have to solve this mystery some other way.*

Kai helped Jay to his feet. Jay pointed at some of the villagers, saying, "Hey, how come they're running *away* from the fire?"

"Let's find out," said Kai, as he stopped one of the villagers. "What's going on? Why aren't you helping?"

"Haven't you heard?" the villager replied. "Skeleton warriors have been seen in the woods near here. We have to get ready to defend ourselves!"

Before the ninja could get any more information, the man rushed off. A moment later, a short, fat man hurried over to where they stood. "My name is Soon," he said. "I

am the elder of this village. I know you are just visitors here, but I have heard that you serve Sensei Wu. Will you help to protect our village from the skeletons?"

"Of course," said Jay. "We haven't **risked our lives** in at least twelve hours. Just show us where they are."

Soon led the two ninja to where about a dozen men from the village were assembled. The skeletons were in the forest just outside of town, and Jay could see there were a lot of them. They were moving through the woods, parallel to the village's main street. So far they hadn't made any hostile moves, but if they launched a raid, the town's defenders wouldn't stand a chance.

Jay, Kai, and the villagers followed the skeletons as they moved. The enemy paused only once, near the ruins of Lee's store. Then they fell into a loose formation as if they were getting ready to attack.

"What will we do?" said Soon. "Lee gave

us about a dozen swords and shields so we could protect the village, but we can't fight so many skeletons. We're doomed!"

"No, we're not. I have an idea," said Jay. "I need some tools, some big metal cans, and a lot of pipe. Can you find that?"

Soon turned to two men. "Hurry and find what the ninja needs."

When the villagers returned, Jay set to work. He punched holes in the cans and fed the ends of the long, thin pipes into them. Then he positioned the cans in trees on either side of where the defenders stood. Each can was about one hundred yards from the group.

"What are you doing?" asked Kai, bewildered.

"Watch and see," Jay said, grinning. "Now I need the men with the loudest voices."

Four men immediately raised their hands.

"Okay, now take the ends of the pipes," Jay continued, "and make as much noise

as you can into them. Yell, shout, bang your swords on your shields, whatever you can think of."

"I don't understand," said Soon. "How does this help us fight off the skeletons?"

"You'll see," Jay said. "Or, rather, you'll hear."

The men did as they were asked, making an enormous ruckus into the ends of the pipes. Instantly, the sounds they were making **boomed** out of the trees. It sounded like there was a whole mob of villagers assembled instead of just a handful.

"That's . . . that's amazing!" exclaimed Soon.

"The sound travels down the pipes and gets amplified by the big cans," Jay said. "By putting the cans on either side of us and a good distance away, it made it seem like there was a big crowd here, all spread out. Look."

The skeletons were moving farther into

the woods, away from the village. Whatever they had come for, they evidently weren't prepared to take on the big group of defenders they thought was assembled nearby.

"Wonderful! Thank you very much!" said Soon, slapping Jay on the back. "What can we do to repay you? Just name it."

"Well," said Jay, "how about the answers to some questions?"

CHAPTER 5

Jay and Soon went to sit on a bench and talk. Kai excused himself, saying he was going to find Lu and ask him some questions of his own. Jay noted that Soon seemed uncomfortable, but having skeletons planning a raid on your village will do that. "What do you want to know?"

"You said Lee 'gave' you swords and shields so your men could defend the town," said Jay.

"Not really 'gave,'" Soon said, looking down at the ground. "More like 'sold,' for quite a bit of money. Our whole treasury . . . we're ruined,

you see. But it was that or face the skeletons with no weapons but shovels and hammers."

"And he only sold you a dozen swords and shields?" asked Jay.

"That's right."

But he had way more than that, thought Jay. *Swords, shields, armor, he bought all of that, but had no record of selling it. A little went to the village—where did the rest go?*

An unsettling thought struck Jay. "Sir, have you had **skeleton raids** on your village before?"

Soon thought for a moment. "No, I can't say we have. Oh, they've been seen in the woods from time to time, but they've never attacked. We don't have much worth stealing."

"Or anything they *needed* to steal," said Jay.

"Isn't that the same thing?"

"No," said Jay, frowning. "It's not."

"At least the skeletons have gone," said Soon. "That's something."

"Gone? No, they're still out there. They're waiting until dark," said Jay. "That's not what my friend Kai would do—he would **charge** right in, regardless of the opposition. Zane would analyze the situation and maybe take action next week. And Cole would spend the whole night planning for an attack tomorrow. Me? I'd do just what the skeletons are going to do: sneak in. I'm a ninja. We're good at sneaking."

Suddenly, Mrs. Park came running towards the men, waving her arms and shouting. She was followed by Kai and Lu.

"In all my years working at the inn, I have never seen such a thing!" she yelled. "Right in broad daylight, too! And where were the village 'defenders'? Playing in the woods!"

"What happened?" Kai asked Mrs. Park.

"It's Din. He was just returning to the inn when three skeleton warriors grabbed him and dragged him off into the woods. He tried

to defend himself, but . . . Well, we found this on the ground."

Lu handed Kai the dagger Din had been holding earlier. He turned it over in his hands, paying particular attention to the blade. As a blacksmith, Kai had seen many swords and daggers before and had a good eye for their shape and quality. "Can I keep this?" he asked.

"Will it help find Din?" asked Lu. He turned to Jay for an answer.

"Oh, he'll be found before tomorrow, don't worry," Jay replied. "I promise, and I always keep my promises. Just ask my friend Cole. Well, no, maybe you better not ask him; I still owe him money. Ask Zane — I never made him any promises, so I haven't broken any."

"Lu, you said there were stories you couldn't share," said Kai. "I think it's time to share them with us."

The tales were about what the ninja

expected to hear—Lee was suspected of being disloyal to the village. A few people reported seeing crates brought into the shop during the night, only to see no sign of them in the morning. The theory was Lee had sold whatever was in them to thieves, perhaps in return for some of their loot. Lu had been robbed several times on the road and lost a great deal of money and goods, and he was certain Lee had profited from his misfortune.

"Why wasn't something done about this?" asked Jay.

"There was no proof," said Lu. "Just suspicion."

Kai turned and walked away with Jay. "I have a suspicion of my own," Kai said quietly. "The skeletons are going to strike again, and we need to make sure they succeed."

CHAPTER 6

Lu, Kai, and Jay headed to Lee's house. Once there, Kai walked over to the trees. He took Din's dagger and seemed to be poking the trunks with it in various places. After a few minutes, he beckoned Lu to come closer.

"See?" Kai said, pointing to the largest of the trees. "I noticed when I was here before that there were all these little Xs carved in the bark of this tree, and a few others. The blade of this dagger is just the right size to have made those marks."

"So you think Din has been attacking Lee's trees?" said Lu. "What for?"

"No, not attacking them," replied Jay. "Right, Kai? He's been using them as a way to contact Lee."

Lu looked up at the setting sun. "The day is almost over. What are you going to do now?"

Kai smiled. "Well, we've talked to you, Mrs. Lee, Mr. Soon, and Din's not available."

"So, naturally, we're going to go talk to the skeletons," said Jay.

After Lu left, Kai took Jay aside. "You handle the spy mission. We both know where the skeletons are heading tonight, so I am going to set up **a little surprise** for them."

Darkness was spreading over the village as Jay slipped into the woods. It was times like these he was really glad not to be his friend Zane. A white ninja robe like he wore made it very hard to be stealthy, unless you were in a snowfield. Dark blue, on the other hand, was made just for the job.

Of course, even with a dark ninja robe, the task was still difficult. Jay couldn't make his appearance known to the skeletons, or he might discourage them from striking that night. That was why he was slipping as quietly as he could from tree to tree, trying to avoid the skeleton warriors. He needed to gather information, not **rack up victories**. Jay just hoped the skeletons liked to talk as much as he did.

He spotted a point of light in the trees up ahead. Drawing closer, Jay could see it was a campfire. Although skeletons did not really feel warmth or cold, they were used to living in the underworld, which was a place of molten lava flows. Fire made them feel more at home.

Jay scrambled farther up a nearby tree as quietly as he could. There were about two dozen skeletons down below, but he didn't see Din anywhere. It was a larger group of warriors than would be needed to raid a

village this size. But a raid wasn't really what they had in mind, or so Jay believed.

Of course, if I'm wrong, the town's in a lot of trouble, the ninja said to himself. *And so are Kai and I.*

He recognized two of the skeletons as Nuckal and Wyplash. They were having a conversation not too far from the tree Jay was hiding in.

"We should have just gone in and taken what we wanted," Wyplash growled. "Who cares how many guys they have in that village? We could have beaten them all."

Nuckal shrugged. "I thought the stuff was supposed to be in the woods? Hey, maybe it was and somebody stole it!"

"Don't be so dense," Wyplash snapped. "Didn't you see that the store fell down?"

"Sure, I did," said Nuckal. "But maybe he was using the crates with our stuff in it to keep the roof up, and when he went to move them, the building fell down."

58

Wyplash just glared at Nuckal.

"Hey, it could happen," Nuckal finished weakly.

The two skeletons stared out into the dark woods for a while in silence. Then Nuckal said brightly, "Hey, maybe we should have shops in the underworld!"

"Selling what?" asked Wyplash.

"I don't know. Lava boats, maybe, or skull polish . . . I hate it when my skull looks dull and dingy, don't you?"

Wyplash slapped Nuckal hard on the back. "You know, pal, I once heard this song all about how the head bone was connected to the neck bone."

"So?"

Wyplash leaned in close, so he was skull-to-skull with Nuckal. "So if you keep making stupid comments like that, your head bone *won't* be connected to your neck bone much longer. **Got it?**"

Nuckal nodded rapidly.

Jay decided he had heard enough. It was time to head back to the village. He almost started to climb down the tree when he spotted a pair of beady eyes staring right at him. They belonged to a red-tailed crow, a species known for its fierce protection of its territory, and its very loud screech. Jay glanced up. On the limb just above him was a large nest, no doubt belonging to the crow.

"I was just leaving," the ninja whispered. "Don't mind me."

The crow took a step forward on the branch, then another.

Jay glanced downward. Nuckal and Wyplash were still right underneath him. If the crow gave its cry, they'd definitely look up. Sure, they probably wouldn't spot the ninja right away. But a screaming bird might attract enough attention that Jay would have a hard time escaping the camp.

"Nice crow. Good crow," Jay said under his

breath. "Sweet, polite crow who isn't going to get me killed."

The crow's beak snapped open, as if it were getting ready to speak. *"Sssshhh!"* Jay said. "You'll wake the neighbors!"

The ninja heard a soft peep from above him. Glancing up, he saw the quizzical face of a baby crow staring down at him from the nest. *This just gets better and better,* thought Jay.

He shifted slightly on the branch. Maybe if he leaped to another limb fast enough, the crow would relax. Jay was just about to jump when he noticed something was in his pocket. Fishing in with his hand, he discovered it was the piece of bread he had taken from dinner the night before.

Smiling, he held the bread out to the mother crow. "See? Here's dinner for you and the kid. And remember, don't talk with your mouth full . . . please."

The crow pecked at the piece of bread. It fell from Jay's hand, tumbling toward the

ground, and finally landed at Nuckal's bony feet. The skeleton bent over and picked it up, then looked up toward the tree.

"Wow," said Nuckal. "Dinner just fell from the sky. I didn't know dinner could do that."

"It can't," said Wyplash, his eyes narrowing. "Could be that someone is in the tree, **spying on us**."

There was a rustle in the branches and a loud screech. An instant later, the mother crow came swooping down at Nuckal. Startled, the skeleton dropped the piece of bread. The bird caught it in her beak and flew back up into the branches.

"Ha! There's your spy," laughed Nuckal. "It's just a hungry crow."

"I guess," Wyplash said. "All right, then, let's get ready. It's almost time to move out."

The two skeletons turned and headed back for the center of the camp. Neither noticed the blue-garbed ninja sneaking away into the night.

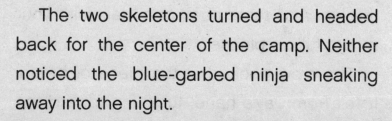

CHAPTER 7

Jay found Kai at the ruined shop. "Been busy?" Jay asked.

"As only I can be," replied Kai.

Jay began rummaging through the ruins of Lee's shop for some odds and ends. He eventually wound up with a metal box and an armful of wires, tools, and various pieces of metal.

"What's all that?" asked Kai.

"I'm going to build a gadget," answered Jay. "It will solve the mystery of who attacked Lee once and for all. Should be ready by morning. But we'd better get in position—

the skeletons are on their way."

Jay was right. No sooner had he, Kai, Soon, and the village's defenders gotten to their hiding places than the skeleton raiding party arrived. As the ninja had suspected, they didn't launch an attack on the village. Instead, they headed for the ruined shop. One by one, they uncovered the crates of supplies and carried them back to the woods.

"Shouldn't we stop them? Shouldn't we attack?" asked Soon.

"No," Jay answered. "They are just taking what they paid for, right? We should let them have it."

"But—"

"Trust me," Jay said with a smile. "Have I ever been wrong?"

"Well, no," Soon admitted. "But then I've only known you a few hours."

In less than ten minutes, the skeletons

were done and had vanished back into the woods. They left one thing behind: Din, tied up, gagged, and sitting in the middle of the ruins. Jay and Kai untied him and brought him back to where the others were waiting.

"Are you all right?" asked Soon.

Din nodded. "They wanted to know how many men were defending the village, but I refused to answer. Once they saw I wouldn't talk, they let me go. But why aren't you going after them?"

An **explosion** rocked the ground, followed by another and another. "That's why," Kai said, grinning. "One of the crates had blasting powder in it. That didn't seem fair somehow, so . . . I made sure all the crates had some."

"So the skeletons are —?"

"Takes more than that to stop skeletons," Kai answered. "But they probably won't be bothering anyone for a while."

"But we still don't know who tried to hurt Lee," said Soon.

"You will in the morning," Jay assured him. "Just get everyone involved in the case together. My little gadget will take care of the rest."

CHAPTER 8

Just after dawn, Jay and Kai had all of the suspects assembled in the town square. Lu and Din both looked wary, Soon seemed angry and uncomfortable, and Mrs. Park just looked tired. Jay cradled his newly built gadget in his arms and looked at them one by one.

"We only came to this town to buy supplies," he began. "But it turned out the general store business is a dangerous one around here. Mr. Lee is still recovering from having the roof fall in, and we came close

to being jailed for attacking him. Somebody went through a lot of trouble to make it look like we did it, and that wasn't very nice."

"So we started investigating," said Kai. "You, Mrs. Park, almost went broke because of the shoddy goods Lee sold you. And you had access to red and blue string—the stuff you were using to make that scarf you were knitting—so planting the threads would have been easy for you."

Jay turned to Lu. "You lost money, too, but in a different way. You got robbed by bandits, thieves you were convinced Lee had supplied. You'd heard of the sensei, and Spinjitzu, and even his tea . . . which made me wonder if you might have met him once, maybe even been trained by him. If that was the case, you could have brought those beams down."

Kai spoke now, looking directly at Din. "You were in business with Lee, weren't you? When you had some extra goods that could be sold to the skeletons, you left a mark for

Lee on one of his trees—a little X. You left one the night he was attacked. That's why he made an excuse to leave the house, so he could go meet you. And that's why his records showed so much more coming in than was being sold. He was selling it to the skeletons. They came last night to collect when they didn't find their crates in the usual spot."

Jay turned to Soon. "Your whole treasury was wiped out by Lee, in return for a measly twelve swords and shields. That was never going to be enough to defend this village—Lee knew it, and you knew it. But he didn't want anyone driving the skeletons away, and you couldn't say no to any offer of help. So you had to pay, no matter how much it hurt."

Kai gave a tight smile. "Four suspects, but only one of you caused the collapse. If we had more time, we could probably find the proof we need, but Jay here promised to

settle this case by this morning. Good thing he's an inventor."

For the first time, everyone paid attention to what Jay was holding. It looked like just a simple metal box with a few wires sticking out here and there. But Jay held it as if it was a golden treasure.

"What is it?" asked Din.

"It's a truth-seeker," said Jay. "I won't bore you with how it works, but it can tell if you're lying or not. To be honest, I already know which of you did this — the clue was in Lee's last word before passing out — but this will give me all the proof I need. So . . . who wants to go first?"

There was a beat of silence. Then Din **broke and ran**. Jay tossed the box to a startled Lu and ran after him.

Din knew the town much better than Jay, and cut between buildings and leaped over fences in an effort to escape. Jay matched

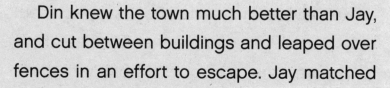

him move for move, then suddenly appeared to give up. Din looked over his shoulder to see the ninja stopped in the middle of the road, wiping his brow and breathing hard.

Din smiled. Ninja, he decided, must be overrated. How else to explain one quitting halfway through a chase? The trader cut left and jogged past the ruins of Lee's shop, heading for the woods. Then he staggered and almost fell at the sight of Kai stepping out from behind a tree up ahead.

"Why waste energy chasing you when we already knew where you had to be going?" Kai laughed. "Now we can do this the hard way, or **the harder way**. Either one will end up with you on the ground."

Din raised his hands, ready to fight. "Go ahead. You have no evidence against me. So I ran — how do I know your friend's stupid machine wouldn't give off some strange rays or something? Maybe you just wanted to get

rid of us so you could get away with something *you* did."

Kai faked a punch with his left and then struck with his right hand, but Din blocked it like an expert. "Strange rays . . . that's a good idea . . . I'll have to tell Jay about that one."

Din executed a perfect lotus dragon kick, but Kai was no longer standing where he had been. He had slipped under the kick and emerged behind his opponent. Kai tapped Din on the shoulder, and when Din turned, he used a sweep kick to knock him to the ground.

"You're good," Kai said. "Fast, even. I can see how you brought those beams down. But where did you get the red and blue thread?"

Din sprang to his feet and rained blows on Kai, who parried each one. Then the trader launched a leaping kick from a standing start, surprising Kai and bowling the ninja over.

"So I did some business with the skeletons. Big deal," Din growled. "They're going to win anyway. Do you really think four ninja and an old man can stop an army?"

Kai rolled at Din, crashing into his legs and bringing his foe down. They struggled in a tangle of arms and legs, neither one getting much advantage over the other. "Got it," said Kai. "You were staying at the inn. All you had to do was borrow some thread from Mrs. Park's knitting."

"Would you be quiet about the stupid thread?" Din snarled, pushing Kai off him.

Suddenly, Jay was behind Din, grabbing his ankle and swinging him into a mound of soft earth. "My turn, Kai. Okay, let's talk about something else, then. Mrs. Lee said her husband's last conscious word was 'traitor.' She heard wrong, didn't she? He didn't say 'traitor'—he said 'trader'—meaning you. What happened? You wanted more

money and Lee didn't want to give it to you?"

Din's face changed into a mask of fury. "All right. Lee was a liar and a cheat. He deserved what he got, and more."

"You should have waited until the skeletons got their goods," Jay said, starting to spin. "They weren't too happy with you. How did you talk your way out of their clutches?"

Din tried to stand up, but Jay had him pinned down. "Okay, okay! I told the skeletons they could get their goods, and get rid of you, plus I would give them their next load of supplies for free. So they let me go."

Jay turned into a **Spinjitzu whirlwind**. The force of the tornado lifted Din off the ground and spun him like a leaf in a storm until he was too dizzy to see straight. Then Jay let him drop unceremoniously into a mud puddle.

Park, Soon, and Lu arrived then, with Jay's gadget in tow. They looked at the ninja, now slowing his spinning to a stop, and then at

the muddy and defeated Din. Soon and Lu grabbed Din by the arms and hauled him to his feet.

"Don't worry," said Soon. "We'll see that he's jailed for his crimes."

"It's too bad you didn't get to use your truth-seeker," said Lu. "I would have enjoyed seeing how it worked."

"I can show you now," said Jay, smiling. "Kai, would you do the honors? Open it up."

Kai pried the box open. Inside there was nothing but a few colored wires, not connected to anything.

"Wait a minute," said Lu. "That's pretty much an empty box. It couldn't detect lies or anything else."

"Really?" said Jay. "Well, Din didn't know that, so I guess it did its job after all."

A few hours later, the ninja had all the supplies they needed loaded on the mules. It would be a long walk back to camp, but they would have quite a story to tell once

they got there. Still, Jay and Kai agreed that they wouldn't mind at all if the next shopping trip was a little less eventful. Just in case it wasn't, Jay decided to start figuring out how to build a real truth-seeker — you never knew when one might come in handy.